TRINITY FIELD REPORT: ALIEN RACES

D1741195

GREETINGS, COLLEAGUE —

In the last few months we've made great strides in xenoscience. First, our studies of the Chromatics captured during the *Eyrie* Station raid were extremely enlightening. We no longer fight this enemy in the dark, as it were. The Chromatics are still a threat to humanity, but although they were once a hostile race with unknown capabilities, they are now beings with measurable strengths and exploitable weaknesses. Armed with this knowledge, Æon is helping the psi orders move ever closer toward the development of effective counter-measures.

Even better, communication with the few living Chromatic captives proceeds apace. Æon Trinity has high hopes that we may negotiate with this fierce alien race — if not find common ground — in the near future. We are confident that humanity could win an out-right confrontation with the Chromatics, but we do not wish to wage a war of attrition.

Among other recent events, the Leviathan *Ananda* has returned from Qinshui, bearing our brave embassy personnel as well as more information on enigmatic Qin culture. The *Ananda* expedition reestablished regular communications between Earth and Qinshui, to the benefit of both.

Humanity and the Qin can now look beyond the mutual concern of returning lost am-bassadors. As I write these words, Qin and human dignitaries meet to renew the techno-logical and commercial negotiations that were interrupted when the Upeo vanished five years ago. We also now know that Aberrant attacks harry Qinshui much as they do Earth. Surely an alliance against our common enemy is at hand.

And finally, even the *second* expedition to the Coalition space ark must be considered a success, despite its violent end. We have no doubt about the Coalition now. The expedition's dramatic discoveries are both shocking and undeniable. Æon Trinity has not yet retaliated, but rest assured that this outrage will be punished.

However, despite our recent discoveries and studies, many details of all three alien races remain a mystery. *Ananda* returned with more questions than answers about the Qin. The puzzle of Chromatic teleportation and biotech remains unsolved. And while we now know more about the Coalition, we still don't know its motives or plans.

Yet, we must keep in mind how little we knew about all three races only a few short months ago. Æon Trinity devotes itself to exploration and discovery, those two essential human pursuits. As long as questions remain about our peers and enemies in space, we will search for answers.

I call upon all Trinity operatives, psion and neutral alike, to share your thoughts, specu-lations and discoveries regarding this field report. You've helped us broaden our horizons further than ever expected. Let us not stop here, but seek out, explore and respond to the challenges that face us. Æon is proud of what you've accomplished — and we are confident that you will continue to surpass the high standards you have set for yourselves.

Ad Astra
Neville Archer
Director, Neptune Division
Æon Trinity
Hope · Sacrifice · Unity

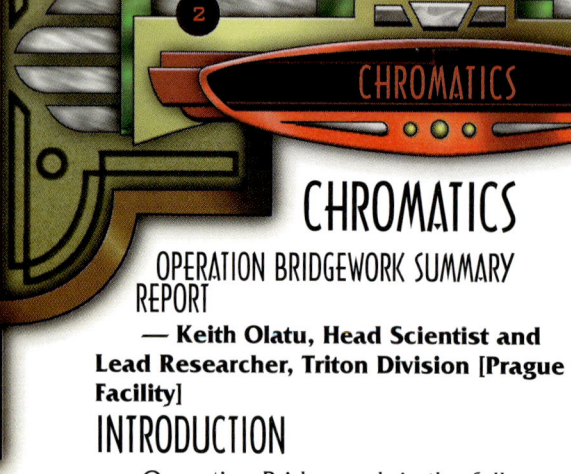

CHROMATICS

OPERATION BRIDGEWORK SUMMARY REPORT

— **Keith Olatu, Head Scientist and Lead Researcher, Triton Division [Prague Facility]**

INTRODUCTION

Operation Bridgework is the follow-up investigation into Chromatic biology, culture and psychology, following the initial Operation Abyss of 2113. Our initial investigation took place in strict isolation on Montressor Clinic grounds, and it was carried out by seven Æon Trinity scientists and appropriate support staff. The Æsculapian Order provided three vitakinetics; Orgotek supplied support both in the form of technical assistance and a single psion expert in photokinetic applications. The Ministry provided two psions skilled in both telepathy and interrogation. The Legions assigned a Sixth Legion strike team in case of hostile attempts on the part of the subjects. The representatives from each order were immensely helpful during the course of our study.

Approximately halfway through the investigation, three UN scientists joined us as observers. Of the three, Mr. Koenig proved to be an inadequate scientist despite a naturally inquisitive nature. The other two scientists were fairly helpful, and they deserve particular credit for their thoughts on Chromatic culture.

The subjects of our investigation are four Chromatics who were captured during the *Eyrie* Station incident that took place in May. We also had access to the full Operation Abyss report [see Proteus Archive, Operation Abyss 7.16.2113] as well as the remains of the Chromatic corpses on which that report was based.

Operation Longjump operated in concert with Operation Bridgework under UN auspices, with the aid of Norça and Nihonjin technicians. Its aim was to analyze all available Chromatic technology, with particular atten-

tion to the aliens' means of travel between the stars. We obtained an abridged version of the Operation Longjump report and we incorporated all relevant material into our analysis. We strongly recommend that further effort be devoted toward obtaining a full copy of the report — this is no time for politics.

The Operation Bridgework team has no final recommendation on the disposal of the Chromatic captives at this time. Two full recommendations are presented under separate covers, but we summarize both at the end of this report.

MEDICAL REPORT

Our medical team confirmed most of the conclusions reached by Operation Abyss. This report addresses only new information and errors in the original report; information from that investigation not specifically addressed should be taken as current and accurate.

The "tubes" running along the Chromatic spine, as discussed in Operation Abyss, are indeed a primarily means of storing energy. However, after much observation, we determined that these tubes are also a secondary element of the Chromatic nervous system. Returning to previous autopsies, we found small eyespots and bioluminescent patches along the insides of the tubes themselves. We further observed that the tubes connect the subjects' sensory and auxiliary brains. As yet, we've developed no procedures to study these arteries in a living subject, but the presence of internal light-producing and sensing organs suggests that these tubes are conduits, speeding the Chromatic equivalent of nervous impulses. This system also explains the reflexes of the average Chromatic warrior, which are significantly faster than those of most human beings.

We chose Chromatic Subject D (a.k.a. Heavystone — see the section on Chromatic culture) for an experiment to determine if Chromatics possess the capacity for osmotic absorption of oxygen in liquids, as postulated by Operation Abyss. During this experiment, Ministry agent Xin Chao probed Heavystone

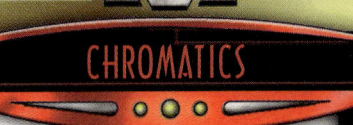
CHROMATIC BIOSCHEMATIC

SENSORY BRAIN

BIOLUMINESCENT "EYESPOT"

SPINAL CORD

AUXILIARY BRAIN

ENERGY/IMPULSE CONDUITS

BINOCULAR EYE

STOMACH/ DIGESTIVE SYSTEM

LUNGS

WIDE ANGLE EYE

MOUTH

GRIPPING CLAW

MANIPULATIVE TALON

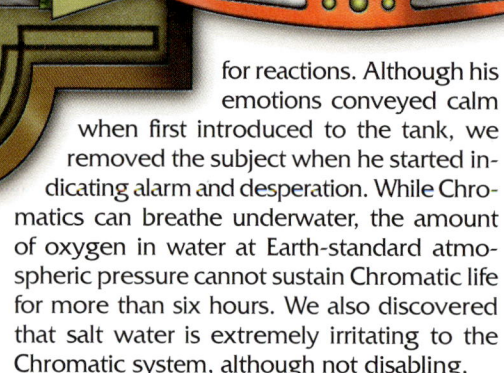

for reactions. Although his emotions conveyed calm when first introduced to the tank, we removed the subject when he started indicating alarm and desperation. While Chromatics can breathe underwater, the amount of oxygen in water at Earth-standard atmospheric pressure cannot sustain Chromatic life for more than six hours. We also discovered that salt water is extremely irritating to the Chromatic system, although not disabling.

The Chromatic ability to store energy and absorb oxygen via osmosis suggests that these creatures live in a resource-poor environment. Given the sensitivity of their numerous eyespots, we suspect that their planet is far from their sun or that they spend a great deal of time isolated from sunlight. The latter seems more likely, as their energy-absorption capabilities are attuned to absorbing solar energies comparable in strength to those from our sun.

Our living subjects belong to two distinct genders, one of which we arbitrarily designated as "female." Chromatic Subject C (a.k.a. Fastswimmer) referred to having "not yet made a small beacon," thus naming herself of that gender, though whether she is too young or otherwise incapable of producing offspring is unclear.

NOETIC REPORT

Chromatics prove to be strong manipulators of noetic fields. Vitakinetic examination indicated that all captives are capable of photokinesis, with some potential for electromanipulation and pyrokinesis. The subjects do not exceed human psion potential. However, our analysis of battlefield reports leads us to believe that Chromatic warriors do *outperform* psions, producing effects the orders consider impossible.

It seems that the Chromatic ability to become invisible and to project illusory images are only partially noetic in nature. They use photokinesis to create images that screen the aliens from view or that make them appear elsewhere. However, the fine control needed to create truly convincing illusions depends on the immense processing power of the Chromatic sensory brain and the network of optical receptors that feed the brain information. At this time, we conclude that psions cannot master the coordination needed for Chromatic-style illusory images.

We nonetheless recommend that the Æon Trinity share our more detailed report on Chromatic aptitudes with Orgotek for further study. Orgotek psions should be able to make use of Chromatic techniques given sufficient practice. The Orgotek assistant to Project Bridgework was very enthused about the possibilities.

By request of Operation Longjump, we investigated the possibility of Chromatic teleportation. We found no trace of psionic teleportation latency — or of any aptitudes beyond those already discussed.

LINGUISTIC REPORT

Although Chromatics do not possess any degree of telepathic ability, they show a formidable resistance to probes. The two Ministry agents used telepathy to gain data initially, but they found that it was difficult to force a Chromatic's thoughts down any one path. Surprisingly, the aliens quickly grew sensitive to such attempts. Whenever one of the Chromatic subjects felt a telepathic probe, it responded with overwhelming feelings of anger and outrage. Xin Chao explained that the aliens seemed to feel that we were not "worthy" to communicate with them in such a fashion.

We are confident that we can break through the aliens' emotional defense, but doing so could harm the subjects' psyches and would be draining on our telepaths. We decided to attempt translating the Chromatics' speech instead.

We are pleased to report that, having so decided, we established communications with the captive Chromatics much more quickly than anticipated. As per earlier speculation, Chromatics use sound to communicate in a limited manner, while their main mode of communication is visual. A specific set of wavelengths, at the limits of human visual perception, carries linguistic content. Interestingly, projectors and sensors of these wavelengths operate on an entirely different set of nerves than does the rest of Chromatic visual perception. We suspect that Chromatics perceive "photo-communication" as something rather different from sight.

(We would like to thank Orgotek and the Ministry for helping us construct a device capable of interpreting and duplicating Chromatic light-communication patterns. We recommend that the United Nations be encouraged to subsidize the production of more translator devices, whether from Orgotek or from another appropriately tractable biotech company. We will need these devices if we ever expect to establish terms with the Chromatics.)

The aliens' language is surprisingly simple for a spacefaring race, despite earlier speculations to the contrary. Their set of basic nouns is approximately one third of the size of the average sets in Earth languages, and one-quarter of the size of the set of Qin basic nouns. However, the language makes extensive use of compound nouns. Very few of these compound nouns are abbreviated to form new constructions.

This pattern applies to Chromatic verb forms as well. Adverb and adjective prefixes build on a small set of verbs to create complex action statements. For example, the verb "to go" is modified by prefixes meaning "quickly," "far," and "high" to form the verb indicating space flight. The multitude of compound verbs and nouns in the Chromatic language seems to have misled previous researchers to believe that the language was complex.

Dr. Haller postulated that the speed with which Chromatics communicate may have reduced evolutionary pressure to condense compound word forms. While we must accept this idea as a possibility, the majority opinion differs. The Chromatics' language is richest when used to speak of light and other optical phenomena, while a secondary locus

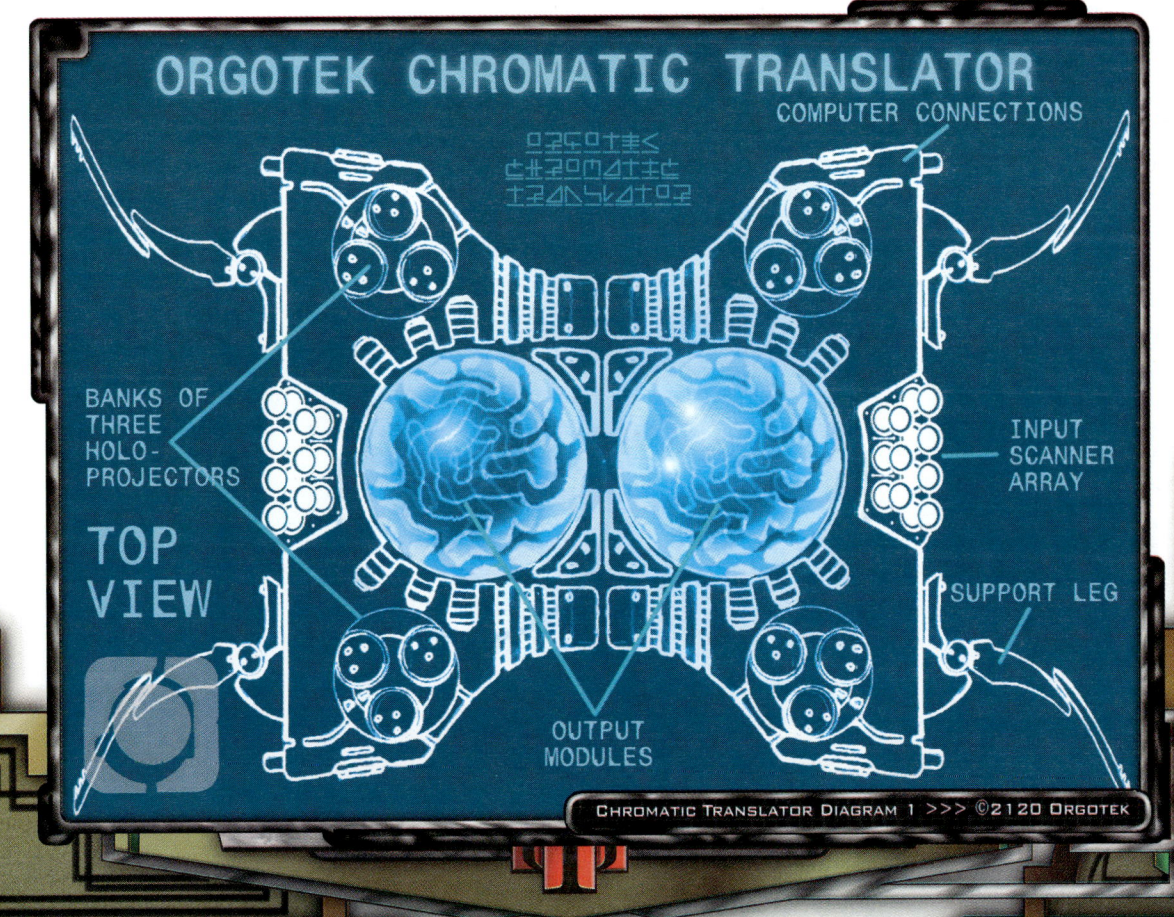

ORGOTEK CHROMATIC TRANSLATOR

COMPUTER CONNECTIONS

BANKS OF
THREE
HOLO-
PROJECTORS

INPUT
SCANNER
ARRAY

TOP
VIEW

SUPPORT LEG

OUTPUT
MODULES

CHROMATIC TRANSLATOR DIAGRAM 1 >>> ©2120 ORGOTEK

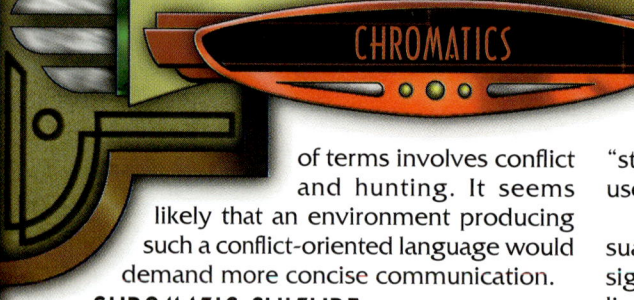

of terms involves conflict and hunting. It seems likely that an environment producing such a conflict-oriented language would demand more concise communication.

CHROMATIC CULTURE

The xenocultural team thanks the linguistics researchers for their contributions to this report; we would never have been able to learn as much as we have without understanding some of Chromatic language. (Note that the translations provided in this report are rough at best. We require many more months of intensive research to refine our understanding of the Chromatic language.)

At first the subjects would not cooperate; they ignored our questions for the first week. We achieved a breakthrough when Dr. Gilman, in frustration, asked Chromatic Subject A (later designated Roamer) how she could convince them to talk. After some apparent thought, Roamer asked Dr. Gilman to "state the truth" that answers would not be used to harm the Chromatic race.

While we're not sure, we think the visual patterns that overlaid Roamer's reply signified skepticism — that they did not believe we are capable of such terms. After consultation with her colleagues, Dr. Gilman agreed to Roamer's request. After lengthy discussion among the subjects — and much to our surprise — the result was notably higher levels of cooperation. It seems that Chromatic culture is highly social. We postulate that our captives may have suffered from something not unlike the Stockholm syndrome observed in human hostages.

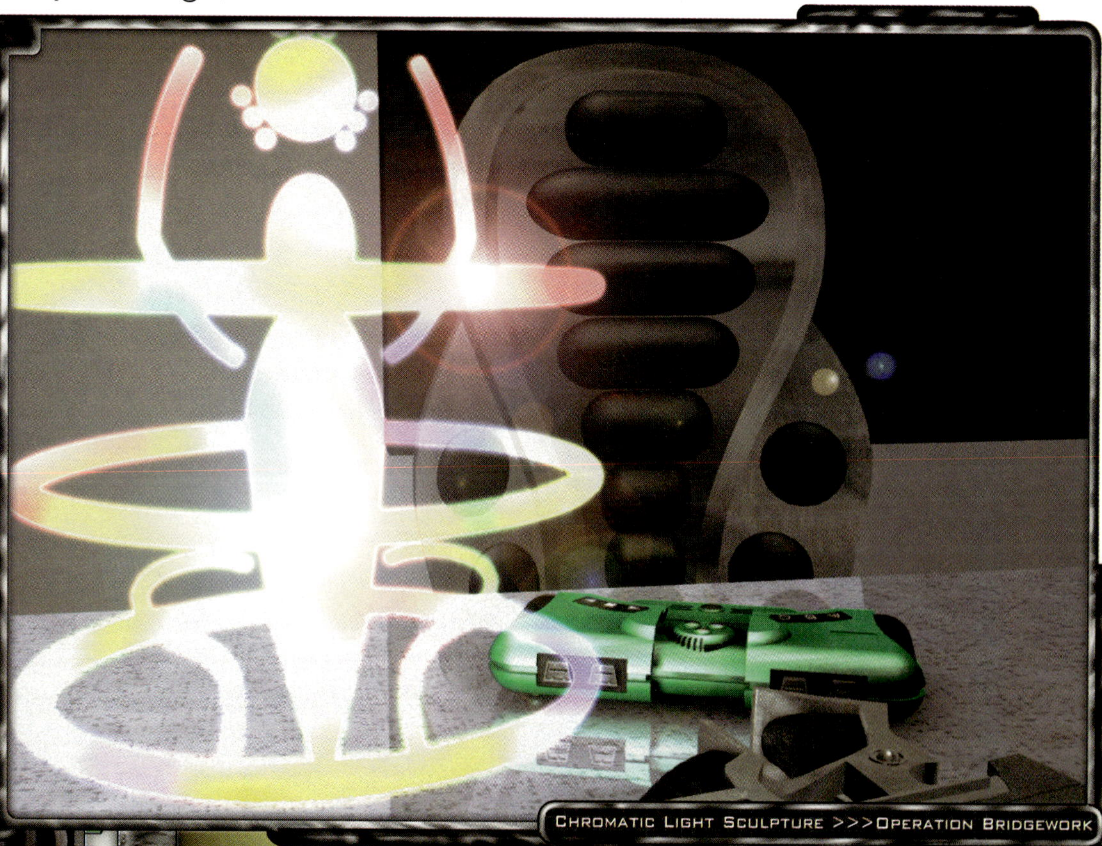

I must stress that this observation does not mean that we believe friendships have developed between the aliens and ourselves. They continue to refer to us as "beasts," and they often unleash violent outbursts in response to what we assume are innocuous comments. The process is touch and go, but

CHROMATIC LIGHT SCULPTURE >>>OPERATION BRIDGEWORK

the simple fact that we have started a dialogue gives us hope.

The social aspects of Chromatic culture revolve around what we characterize as spiritualism. Understanding the nature of their "religion" is frustratingly difficult. Their entire mythological structure is subject to frequent revision. While there is a priesthood among the Chromatics, they consider spiritual revelations and insights valid no matter who experiences them. Furthermore, such "insights" spread at amazing speeds. There are indications that the priesthood varies in membership, consisting of those who recently experienced significant revelations.

Apparently there are times when two mutually incompatible beliefs coincide. This is one cause of intra-Chromatic conflict. According to our subjects, the current battle against humanity is the result of such a struggle, apparently involving a new brand of polytheism. Other causes of conflict include struggles for resources. It is interesting that the stories we were told revolved around conflicts over food and living space, rather than for natural resources such as mineral ores.

Further discussion revealed that Chromatic existence is largely subterranean, as per the medical team's speculation. Chromatics consider water to be a precious substance found only underground. Existence is more dangerous there due to predation and the rare geological instability, but it is also more rewarding. "Watering holes" are the most strongly desired territories, because they ensure a supply and because Chromatic prey requires water just as much as the aliens themselves do. These findings seem to indicate that Chromatic culture is still in the hunter-gatherer phase.

One of the most revealing aspects of Chromatic culture is the Chromatics' method of choosing names. Young Chromatics are born with no names, and they are identified with generic pronouns. Adults often give the young simple descriptive terms for the sake of distinguishing them, but these terms are shed as soon as the young one acquires a "real" name.

A nameless Chromatic earns a name by distinguishing itself, where the name reflects the deed that gained the young Chromatic recognition. For example, Heavystone gained his name after single-handedly scattering an enemy position by rolling several rocks of extraordinary size down into the enemy's ranks. A Chromatic chooses his own name, although it is subject to group consensus, in case, for example, it is overly egotistical.

As evidenced by Longeye Underhider's name (a.k.a. Chromatic Subject B), Chromatics can earn more than one name. This practice is, however, considered somewhat arrogant. Chromatics tend to leave the most glorious moments to those who have not yet earned a name. We theorize that this tradition is a cultural adaptation to the risky life the race appears to lead. If the youngest Chromatics seek out the greatest risks in order to name themselves, then the wisdom of the elders, who have already earned their names, is less likely to be lost.

Our current sample of Chromatic names includes Heavystone, Longeye Underhider, Roamer and Fastswimmer. While this selection is very small, it is undeniably inclined toward physical accomplishment. Furthermore, the "name stories" we have heard suggest a violent and warlike culture. We are unable to reconcile this finding with the fact that the Chromatics are a spacefaring race. We cannot construct a cultural model that allows for both primitive warfare and spaceships.

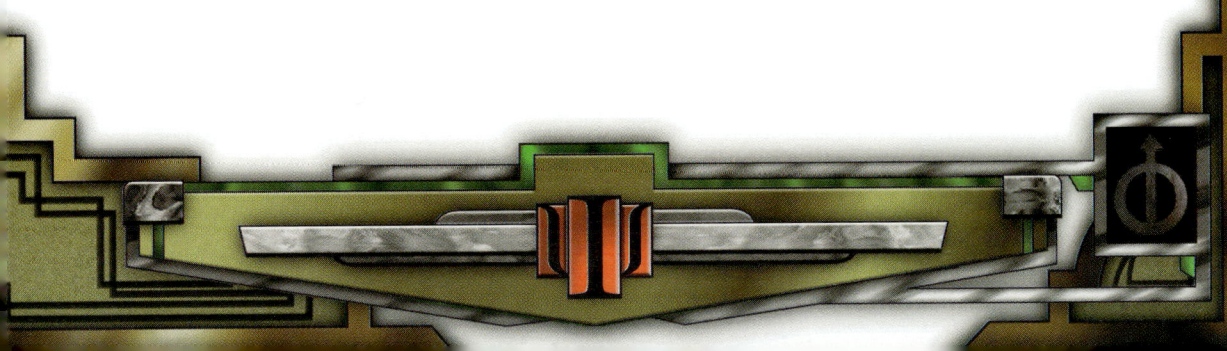

OPERATION LONGJUMP SUMMARY

— Jaqui Rodriguez, UN Lead Administrator, Operation Longjump

We began our analysis of Chromatic biotech with as few suppositions as possible. Three of our staff members were unaware of the source of the biotech at the beginning of the study; we told them its origin was unknown. We took all necessary precautions to avoid influencing their analysis of the biotech. They were a control group, if you will.

Both the control group and the main group concluded that the biotech was based on old human designs, with modifications from an unknown source. The DNA used, however, is closely related to Chromatic DNA, and we can assume that it originates from various species on the Chromatic homeworld. While the bioapps' external interfaces were arranged in ways that the control group termed "unsuitable for human use," the underlying components were exceedingly similar to basic human designs. In many cases, they were identical.

Interestingly, we found no signs of Qin influence. Qin biotech is extremely distinctive and, generally speaking, more advanced than our own — it would not be possible to miss it. On a hunch, we cross-referenced the recognizable human designs with records of biotech patents. No available Chromatic biotech is based on Orgotek designs more recent than 2108 — at which time Qin biotech was not widely available on Earth.

On the issue of space travel: We have no idea how the Chromatics reached either Earth's orbit or Karroo. Our Solar System is well-monitored by both technological and noetic means, and there was no sign of Chromatic ships approaching in normal space before the attack on *Eyrie* Station.

There was some fear that the Chromatics use a form of the Aberrant warp ability, but noetic monitoring prior to the raid registered nothing. We also investigated debris from the raid for indications of taint. Much to our relief, we discovered no such signs.

However, noetic monitoring *did* detect a localized subquantum wave indicative of psionic teleportation. It is obvious that the Chromatics have some means of teleporting, but we do not know how they do it. We understand from Operation Bridgework reports that the Chromatics bear no signs of teleportation capabilities, nor do the subjects themselves seem to understand the principles involved.

We then re-examined Chromatic biotech, hoping to discover something like Tesser jump-engine technology. This avenue of investigation has thus far proven inconclusive. (We would like to perform a third examination with Qin aid, which was not possible at this time due to the alien ambassadors' return to Qinshui.)

Finally, while reviewing Operation Bridgework notes on Chromatic religion, we noticed that the Chromatic captives associate both cold and absolute darkness with malevolence. We questioned them further on this subject and confirmed that our captives fear space itself. Indeed, they pride themselves on surviving space travel. As Roamer put it, "We braved >>> death? total blackness? <<< and brought our light safely through." This incongruity raises the question of what inspired the Chromatics to venture into space in the first place?

While we apologize for our lack of information, we hope that the questions we have raised are helpful.

RECOMMENDATIONS

While both Operations Bridgework and Longjump were undeniably successful, they leave us with many questions. It seems clear that Chromatic culture, as our captives have described it, is not sufficiently advanced to create the kind of biotech that the Chromatics possess. What is perhaps worse is that much of it bears a frightening similarity to human biotech.

The issue of teleportation remains completely opaque. While Operation Bridgework speculates that some sort of caste or gender-based division exists in Chromatic noetics — suggesting that there may be a group of teleport-capable aliens we have yet to encounter — we have not confirmed this suspicion despite extensive interviews with our subjects.

As scientists, we are reluctant to draw conclusions without strong evidence, particularly in matters so vital to the human race. However, we must admit that the majority of our evidence points toward external influence on the Chromatics. We urge that Æon Trinity operatives be made aware of this possibility. If it is true, we must consider the danger of yet another life form at work in the universe as we know it, a culture seemingly ill-disposed toward humanity — at least for now.

Finally, we cannot afford to rule out the possibility that the Chromatics are an artificial race. Despite intensive probes, many of our questions could not or would not be answered. While the aliens are undeniably sentient, they are not overly intelligent. Are Chromatics biological constructs of some sort? If so, who created them?

REPORT: TELEPATHIC PROBE OF CHROMATICS

— Xin Chao, Ministry of Psionic Affairs, Office of Semiotics [detached duty to Operation Bridgework]

I have performed only very limited telepathic interrogation, as it seems unwise to incite the Chromatics. Operation Bridgework currently holds the captive Chromatics with the modern equivalent of spit and baling wire; the strongest component of their captivity is the Chromatics' belief that they are held securely. (Fortunately, they are willing to believe assertions that the area in which they are being held is inescapable.) I chose not to give them reason to test their cells.

My telepathic scans were most successful when the Chromatics were in darkness and asleep. I scanned at surface levels and received little more than dream impressions. I am unable to resolve the most pressing question: the matter of teleportation. However, their dreams show only the most cursory thoughts of technology. While reading alien dreams is perhaps the very definition of an inexact science, it does not seem that the subjects live on a technological world. On the other hand, dreams of a religious nature (tentatively polytheistic, with multiple "gods of light") are exceedingly common.

Preliminary hypothesis: Chromatic society is highly segregated. Warriors, such as the subjects in captivity, are deliberately kept in a primitive environment for unknown reasons. In my capacity as Ministry representative, I suggest that future military expeditions should endeavor to capture a Chromatic of the technological caste. This group could possibly attempt to do so in the guise of a religious order of some kind, as the Chromatics may be more receptive to that approach.

Qin

— Journal, Maria Diaz, Junior ISRA Representative, First Qinshui Expedition

March 21st, 2115

I always thought people who kept diaries were too caught up in themselves. Who wants to read about ordinary people doing ordinary things in ordinary times? I never thought something extraordinary might happen to me, but even if I'd expected something extraordinary, I'd never have predicted a disaster like this.

Some folks say that Earth must have been destroyed, that the Aberrants wrecked it. I can't believe that.

But regardless, here I am, sitting on Qinshui the year after the Upeo stopped coming, and I realize that if I ever get out of this I'll want to remember what it was like at the time. As much as I hate to say it, if I don't get out of this, maybe this journal will prove useful to Earth when humanity finally does get back here.

So here it is. To my future self, if it's me reading this: Don't ever give up. When you were my age, you promised yourself that. And if this is someone else — thank you for coming for us, and don't blame yourself if it was too late.

>>> Approximately 176 kilobytes of entries deleted <<<

May 12th, 2119

It's a bit of a pain being a backup. Most of the staff members have a primary and secondary function, so everyone's someone else's

fail-safe, as well as having a main job. It's a good system. My gripe is that psions have to spend enough time mastering their powers — there's not a lot of spare time to learn any other specialty. I'm a pretty good clairvoyant, but I haven't had time to learn enough about anything else to do it full time, which makes me the professional basketweaver around here.

Not that I should complain, being on mankind's greatest adventure and all, but people are people no matter what. There's a betting pool on what the Qin really look like. I have five yuan on something six-legged and furry. See what I mean? Something as important as that, and I'm making bets on it.

Anyway. I've been trying to think of silver linings to our exile. I've already seen more marvels than I would have in a lifetime on Earth. This place is like a fairyland. I was told

the Qin were masters of biotech, but seeing what that means on a planetary scale is completely different.

Everything here is organically grown instead of manufactured. The buildings remind me of termite mounds. They're domes and tubes, shaped out of some sort of glassy substance. It might be chitinous. I'm always restraining the urge to chip some off and find out. The colors are great, almost anima. Kostbaar would love this place. The overall color scheme is muted pastel, but you get an outburst of vibrant purple or green here and there.

It rains all the time. The colors are like a reminder that the rain isn't the only thing in the world. Like I said, very anima.

Josuke Yoshi, one of my friends in the diplomatic corps, talks about how he never expected biotech to be so harmonious. I was surprised Nippon sent someone along, given how

QIN CAPITOL > SOUTH VIEW FROM EMBASSY >>> ÆON ARCHIVE

they feel about non-hardtech, but politics demands a representative. He's a lot happier here than I would have expected. He's also very fond of Qin discussions, which are very elliptical — oblique. He says it's refreshing to deal with a society that's as polite as the Nihonjin, but in a different way.

>>> Approximately 720 kilobytes of entries deleted <<<

December 9th, 2119

Slugs. Would you believe it? A meter long or so — and ugly!

I got tired of sitting around. Jennifer is doing all the probes. She says she doesn't want me to risk pushing too hard and offending our hosts. It's actually pretty cool of her, but it leaves me bored. So I got together with the guys in Engineering who were running the betting pool, and a few of us —Roberts, Sandoz and I — snuck out of the official embassy area. Not very risky. In the last three years, I'd gotten a good handle on the Qin noetic signature, so I figured I could keep us out of sight.

We struck out about half a kilometer outside the human quarter, in the direction that most of their ornithopters head. There was a big dome there with 'thopters landing inside it, and there they were — slugs going in or coming out of those tubes of theirs.

They're a meter or so long, colored mostly in grays and tans and other earth tones, with stripes of brighter colors here and there. They have segmented bodies and what look like little treads that propel them across the ground. I could make out tentacles below what might have been a mouth. One of them was carrying something in its tentacles! I had to restrain myself from laughing; to see these things for the first time after so long — no wonder they wear those suits around us.

Anyhow, after a few minutes of gawking we headed back to the human quarter. An ornithopter came close to noticing us, but I don't think it did. Laura

wanted to file a report, but Jerome and I convinced her it was a bad idea. Ambassador Flores is serious about respecting Qin privacy, especially now that we've lost contact with Earth. That makes sense — if we anger the Qin, we have absolutely nowhere to go. I'll let the cat out of the bag if we ever get home again.

>>> Approximately 25 kilobytes of entries deleted <<<

December 16th, 2119

The pilot of that ornithopter *did* spot us, but it's turned out to be a good thing after all. There's quite a bit we didn't know about Qin society, and I think it's important stuff. I'm now making some of the most interesting discoveries of the entire mission. If I had to take a few risks to make it happen, I don't mind. I just wish I could get word back to Earth.

A week after our "outing," I was contacted by Meizhu, the superior of the Qin pilot who saw us outside the ambassadorial zone. Meizhu has invited me to meet with him on several occasions now to, as he (I think) puts it, "discuss our home." I don't know why I've been singled out, but Meizhu says our head ambassadors already know everything he's telling me.

These are translations, so they might not be exact. There are five, "houses" or political groups in Qin society. Since it's a spacefaring society, they're all basically working toward the same goal, but there are exceptions. They're not nations but they compete like countries do on Earth. The different houses fill different roles in society.

SKETCH FROM JOURNAL OF MARIA DIAZ >>> 12.9.2119

They're kind of a cross between political parties and psi orders. Well, that's not quite right, but it'll do for now.

Meizhu is from House Hsiao Kuo (you can thank China's first contact for that; about half of these houses were named using the I Ching). Apparently all the Qin who've had extended contact with us are from House Tung Jen. They're the ones who traditionally take an exploratory role, which is why they met us first, and they've kept a tight lid on us ever since.

Meizhu says that when we established contact with the Qin, House Tung Jen attempted to establish a monopoly on humanity to upset what he calls the "Travel of a Hundred Spheres." (That translates roughly into "political balance.") It makes sense. A race as concerned with biological balance as the Qin naturally has similar views toward politics. Unfortunately, House Tung Jen might upset the entire thing.

I suppose it's pretty normal to try. Meizhu didn't seem upset by it or anything. The only problem is that this kind of effort isn't supposed to succeed; humans are a completely new factor, so the political scales are tipping heavily. Apparently that makes us disruptive.

>>> Approximately 130 kilobytes of entries deleted <<<

January 22, 2120

It's been a busy few weeks. Meizhu has introduced me to a few other members of his house. I've learned a lot about Qin society, but I'm worried that if I tell Ambassador Flores, I'll be ordered to stop. I'm also not sure that the rest of the embassy really has a clear picture of what's going on. It's not like House Tung Jen is morally corrupt or anything, but I think the other houses are ready to join forces against the Aberrants, and are possibly more eager to help us get home, which is the most important thing.

There's one other house called Kuei, which is extremely anti-human. They're influential, but not as much as Meizhu's house. House Tung Jen used to be the most influential, but they put a lot of resources into the diplomatic mission to Earth. When we lost contact with home, the rest of the house was stranded here without its most important members. The rest of Tung Jen is really just using us. I can understand the logic, but not when there's so much more at stake.

· TRITON ARCHIVE ·

Subject: Staff Memorial
From: Ambassador Flores
To: All Qin Embassy staff
Encryption: SPE
Transmission type: textfile
Date: 2.27.2120

Certainly it is a joyous time now that ships from Earth have returned to Qinshui and to our embassy after five years of isolation. We have a great deal to be thankful for, and we all appreciate the hospitable treatment we have received from our hosts.

However, these glad tidings do not come without some sadness. As you know, Junior ISRAn representative Maria Diaz and engineers Laura Roberts and Jerome Sandoz were tragically killed last week while venturing *outside* the official ambassadorial sector. I have personally inspected the accident scene and ordered autopsies of the bodies. Our Qin allies apologize profusely for the accident, and offer their condolences.

Though our loss is terrible, it saddens me most to know that these three young people never had the chance to see their home again.

Summary: Qinshui Expedition

— Bruce Lysik, Æon Trinity Diplomat Plenipotentiary, Qinshui Expedition, 5.17.2120

Neville:

You'll want to read my full report at your leisure, but here's the summary as requested. The full report goes to the UN as well, so we can expect leaks to the press.

The first section covers fauna, flora and other such. There's a lot of detail about ecological issues that you can read if you want. What's important and interesting, I think, is the fact that we clearly identified traces of bioengineering in 87% of the life forms we were able to study, and that we couldn't rule out bioengineering in the remaining 13%. I suspect that the Qin have reworked the entire planet into their own version of Paradise, with no tigers or mosquitoes.

This evidence of reworking betrays an astounding comprehension of biological issues. Qin bioengineering, while beyond our current abilities, is something we've all had the chance to get used to. What surprises us is the Qin talent for ecological management. The web of ecological interactions on Qinshui appears no less complex than that on Earth.

The North American Blight is ample proof to even non-technical me that you can't alter any element of an ecology without sending profound repercussions throughout the entire planet. Even so, the Qin appear to have changed every single element of theirs.

This degree of manipulation raises an interesting possibility; we might want to consider that the planet wasn't the Qin's original habitat. There's no hard proof that Qinshui is really the Qin homeworld. What if the Qin found it and, er, "Qinshuiformed" it? This supposition doesn't seem likely, but it's one for the Implausible Files.

Also note — this isn't in the full report — that the Qin were leery about letting us study their world. Our investigation didn't reveal anything damning, and we did a reasonably good job of getting around their restrictions, so I believe the Qin's concern was simply habitual. They have a distinct tendency to divulge as little as possible. It seems to be part of their lifestyle.

We got the chance to examine one of their fliers after an accident near the human quarter. The examination was regrettably brief, but revealing. The flier wasn't what we think of as biotech, really. While a flier isn't capable of reproduction, Dr. Narayan declared that it possessed every other characteristic of a living organism.

It was very similar in internal structure to the flying creatures we examined. The space that would ordinarily have been filled with gas pockets was occupied by what appeared to be biotech that provided mobility and lift superior to what a gas bag could provide to wildlife. The exterior shell was also separate from the creature itself. We detached a small segment for further tests, and it proved to be chitinous — much like a beetle's shell, but far sturdier. The material is certainly organic in origin.

Oh, and the thing had parasites! So not only do the Qin custom-grow their vehicles as needed, they fit them into the planet's ecology. (Apparently it isn't as difficult as it sounds; the internals of the vehicles are probably the same as the

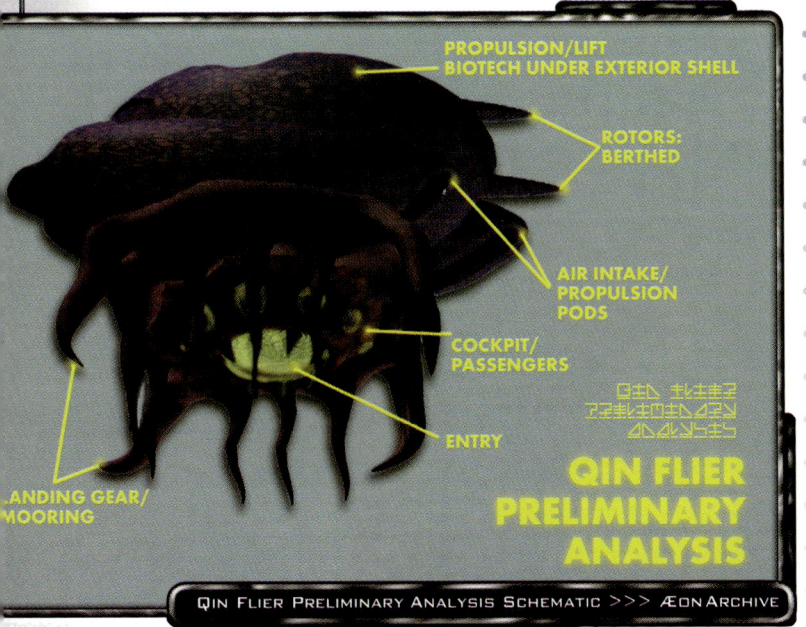

PROPULSION/LIFT
BIOTECH UNDER EXTERIOR SHELL

ROTORS:
BERTHED

AIR INTAKE/
PROPULSION
PODS

COCKPIT/
PASSENGERS

ENTRY

LANDING GEAR/
MOORING

QIN FLIER
PRELIMINARY
ANALYSIS

QIN FLIER PRELIMINARY ANALYSIS SCHEMATIC >>> ÆON ARCHIVE

"native" creatures', with only the outer shells differing. In light of these findings, Dr. Narayan wants to move to Qinshui permanently.)

I get to talk about my field in section three. These folks have ferocious politics; I doubt there's a politician on Earth who couldn't learn something here. So be careful who we send!

Qin society is caste-based, much like old Nippon or India. Unlike those nations, though, each "caste" is also a political entity, and there aren't any real political bodies outside the castes. In other words, after you get over thinking of the Qin as Asian, you realize that they're organized more like the labor unions of the 20th century.

Ambassador Delgado wants the Qin word for their societal divisions translated as "house," but I'm more comfortable with "caste." The groups are oriented more toward function than lineage. Castes are hereditary, but they're defined by what they do. On the other hand, a Qin can't really join a caste other than the one he was born into, so maybe I'm just being stubborn.

The castes interlock as smoothly as the ecology. There isn't a lot of wasted effort on Qinshui. Some jobs are more important than others, but there aren't any totally useless castes as far as I could tell. I'd be very interested to find out what happens to a caste whose role in society becomes obsolete. When I tried to research political history, I ran into that "minimal-information" problem again.

In any case, five or six castes have critical roles. Status is determined within a group economically and by how many other castes pay attention to you. As with societal structures everywhere, the powerful tend to become more so.

Of course, there are always shakeups when something unexpected comes up — like us. One of the castes, the one we call Tung Jen, was right above the middle of the pack when we made First Contact. We had hardtech, which no Qin had ever seriously considered before. We had teleportation. We could have been an incredible gift or an insidious curse. Tung Jen staked its future on us.

The Qin who came back to Earth with us represented the majority of the caste. When we lost the Upeo, the portion of the group left on Qinshui lost most of its power and was apparently in some danger of being absorbed into one of the lesser castes. The Qin back on Earth were clearly aware of this likelihood, which explains

why they were so eager to get back. It wasn't just a matter of being isolated — or it was, but the consequences were farther-reaching than we realized.

We got back just in time, and Tung Jen owes us. Since *Ananda* arrived, things have been humming. Tung Jen still carries some sort of precedent in dealing with us, as "payment" for the risk they took, plus they have the advantage of five years' experience working with our hardtech. I think it's enough to turn their fortunes dramatically, but I talk about that more in the next section.

Section four summarizes our negotiations. Ambassador Delgado was our lead, as per mission assignment, but I kept a close eye on Æon Trinity interests. It's hard to be sure, but it seems to me that Tung Jen is deliberately retarding negotiations until it can solidify its position. Our assistance in getting them back home, not to mention our general value, means the Qin of the Tung Jen caste want to establish strong ties with us — but not just yet.

HSIAO KUO · RECONCILIATION
TUNG JEN · COMMUNITY
KUEI · VIGILANCE

QIN CASTE/HOUSE SYMBOLS

I'm unable to learn a reason for the delay. Aberrants have attacked the Qinjunan system, and Tung Jen has presented us with evidence that one of the other important castes considers us responsible for the Aberrant threat. It's hard to refute this; we are. Maybe Tung Jen can't make a treaty with us until it has enough power to defeat the opposition.

However, I don't think we can overlook the possibility that the treaty will spread the benefits we offer beyond Tung Jen. I can't imagine any treaty restricting human contact to one caste, given how useful we are. (A side note: We shouldn't let that make us egotistical. They're as useful to us as we are to them.) Thus, when a treaty is signed, the Tung Jen caste won't have as much leverage and the time to grab power will have passed. Is that issue of timing a major factor of their plans? They're too good at hiding the truth for me to be sure.

Finally, we come to section five: What do we do now? I'm pretty grateful that it's not my decision. I think we and the Qin need a treaty, but we need one

Analysis: Qin First Contact

The pattern for Qin names was set in haste during humanity's initial contact with the aliens. One of our biggest priorities at the time was adjusting to our first alien race. Rather than convert Qin phonemes into something pronounceable by humans, our diplomats — led by Chinese explorers — decided that the easiest compromise was to give the Qin suitable Chinese names.

Records of initial meetings make it clear that Chua Lianwei carefully guided and shaped the final agreement with the aliens. In retrospect, we should have allowed a naming scheme less reminiscent of China. Although newer Qin designations draw from other cultures, the initial Eastern influence can't help but color human perceptions of the aliens.

We need to be more careful about this sort of bias in the future — we can plan for it in the case of the Coalition, and we should write a general set of nomenclature guidelines for inclusion in the United Nations' current First Contact Manual.

Initial reports from Qinshui indicate that there are multiple nations (or at least multiple political entities) on the Qin homeworld. The first few were given human names drawn from the I Ching. Triton is pursuing further translation of the Qin language to replace these designations with the race's own terms — or to at least apply phonetic variations of the aliens' strange tongue. Despite the fact that the Qin don't seem to care what we call them, we shouldn't risk characterizing the Qin with human national stereotypes. For better or worse, many such problems already exist given the strong Chinese flavor of the Qin public image. At this point it's more important that the public *not* think of the Qin as a Chinese national resource. Check the archives; the number of news articles marking similarities between Qin and Chinese culture is on the rise.

Neptune Division recently finished a plan for implementing multicultural nomenclature. Our staff at the Qinshui embassy will soon begin to discuss the possibility with the other Qin political entities. Back on Earth, Neptune is initiating a subtle media campaign to disassociate Qin culture from Chinese culture. The division may request personnel assistance from Triton and/or Proteus if "freelance" journalism seems in order.

more than they do — and I think they know it.

The Aberrants are a threat to our existence. The Second Aberrant War has only just begun and it's going to get worse before it gets better. While the Aberrants are dangerous to the Qin and have attacked Qin colonies, they simply aren't as threatening from the Qin perspective. Aberrants have a strong reason to come back to Earth, and no reason beyond impulse to attack Qinshui.

The Qin know all this; we couldn't hide it if we tried. Unfortunately, the Qin are a paranoid race. Our embassy personnel stranded here didn't learn nearly as much about their hosts as Qin ambassadors did about Earth. In fact, our information about castes is about all the data we have. So not only are the Qin negotiating from strength, they're negotiating with better information.

My recommendation is that we get down to brass tacks with the Qin of the Tung Jen caste. We gain nothing from pretending that concerns don't exist. Let's be frank with them instead and see where it gets us. We can be more beneficial to their political goals if we're explicitly aiding them. I don't know if helping a specific faction of an alien race is morally correct — but right now, right here, it's necessary.

QIN

COALITION DATAPOD READOUT

Datapod Dump One

— Molly Irvingson, Ambassador in Chief, Second UN Expedition to the Coalition

I'm very pleased to report that our second contact with the Coalition is proceeding much better than the first.

We began cautiously. The Leviathan *Kohl* was detailed to reestablish contact with the Coalition space ark, while her sister ship *Pandora* stood off one Astronomical Unit, with her frigates prepared for hostile action. Only the transport *Chelsea*, just large enough to carry a small embassy, would come into physical contact with the space ark. We stripped *Kohl*'s crew to the minimum necessary to maintain the ship at a standstill, and briefed everyone of the fate of the last expedition.

Kohl's communication officer sent hails ranging up and down the electromagnetic frequency, keeping the power low to avoid any apparent hostility. At 93,604 kilohertz, just inside the FM-radio frequency, he received a reply. It was in English! While the giant Coalition ark stood still, obscuring the Milky [Way and casting our tiny] Leviathan into shadow, the Coalition invited us to dock with its ship and promised to make all possible amends for the horrible misunderstandings that ruined our first contact.

My staff and I transferred onto *Kohl*, and from there, onto *Chelsea*. While *Kohl* maintained position 14 million kilometers away — 10 times closer than *Pandora*, but far enough away to be safe — *Chelsea* docked with the ark. The process was… tense. We did not link airlocks as I expected, but rather entered the space ark proper through an immense portal in her outer hull. I couldn't help but wonder if this was how Jonah felt. *Chelsea* opened her landing doors and we walked out to meet the Coalition.

We were met by a group of mixed race, all naked. I later found that nudity is not necessarily the custom among all races of the Coalition, but that they had chosen to meet us this way to reassure us. There were three members of the race we now call "envoys," accompanied by a number of squat unintelligent-looking four-legged beasts that I've termed "drones." The lead envoy came forward, and in an amazingly mellifluous voice said, "Welcome to our home. We have been poor hosts. While we can never undo what we have done, we hope that together our races can move past this tragedy."

It was odd, but I found the words — typical diplomatic phrasing, in retrospect — reassuring. Perhaps the fact that they had gone to the trouble of learning English made them seem more sincere. I made my greetings, in the name of the United Nations and humanity, and we settled to the task of finding common ground.

(I'm still unsure how the envoys learned English in just seven months, although the Qin learned it in two. We've recognized racially based task-division among Coalition members; I suspect that envoys are particularly adept at linguistic tasks, judging from their grasp of the language. One of our Chinese crew members has volunteered to teach them Mandarin >>> text lost <<<)

We'd made great strides by that evening. Apparently, despite the vast misunderstandings overshadowing our initial contact, the Coalition managed to learn enough by observing Earth's broadcast transmissions from the past two centuries. As the classic novels speculated aliens might, they listened to our broadcasts as they approached Earth — "Realizing," the lead envoy explained, "that entertainment produces an inaccurate picture."

If I understand the envoy's account correctly, sexual contact is considered a normal

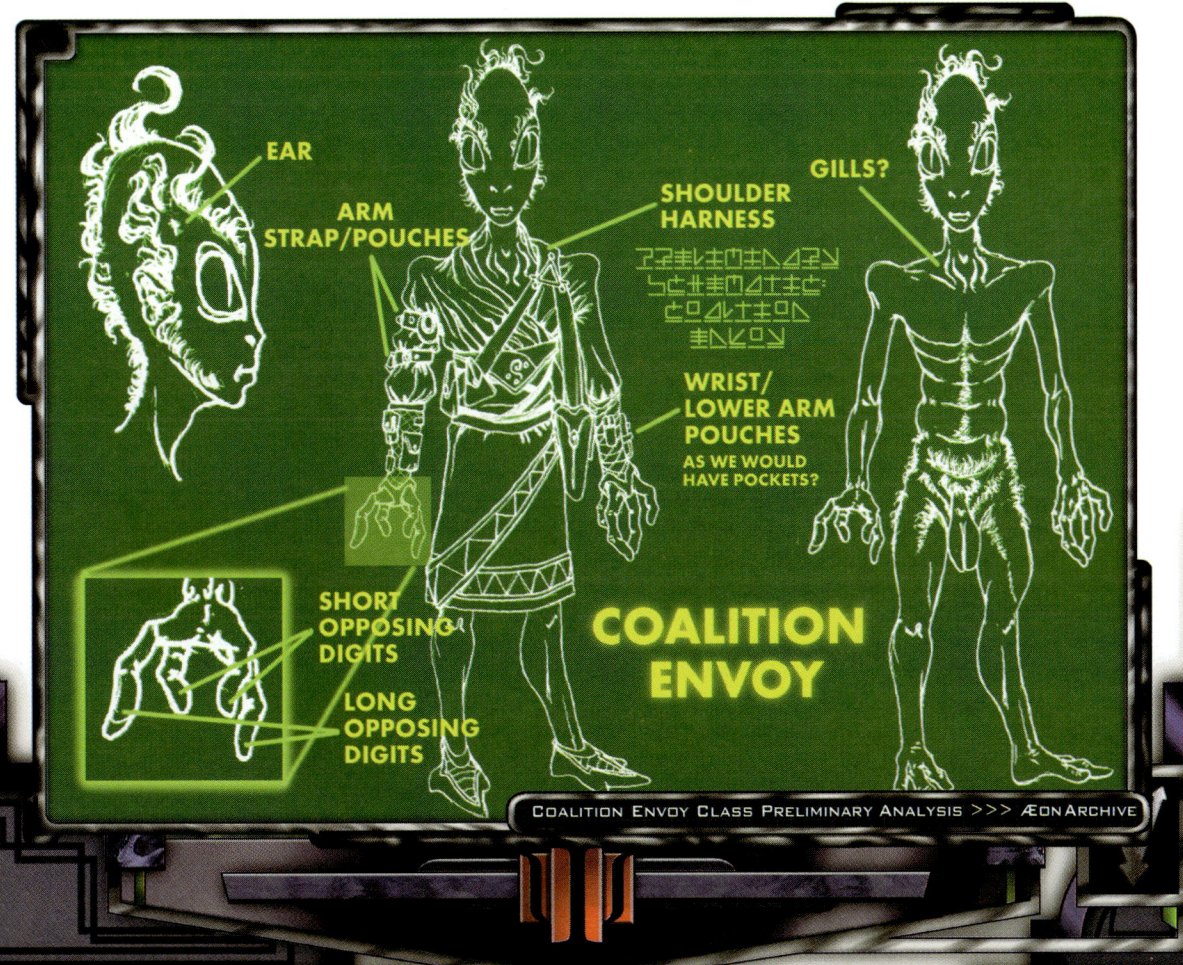

EAR

ARM STRAP/POUCHES

SHOULDER HARNESS

GILLS?

WRIST/ LOWER ARM POUCHES
AS WE WOULD HAVE POCKETS?

SHORT OPPOSING DIGITS

LONG OPPOSING DIGITS

COALITION ENVOY

COALITION ENVOY CLASS PRELIMINARY ANALYSIS >>> ÆON ARCHIVE

COALITION DRONE

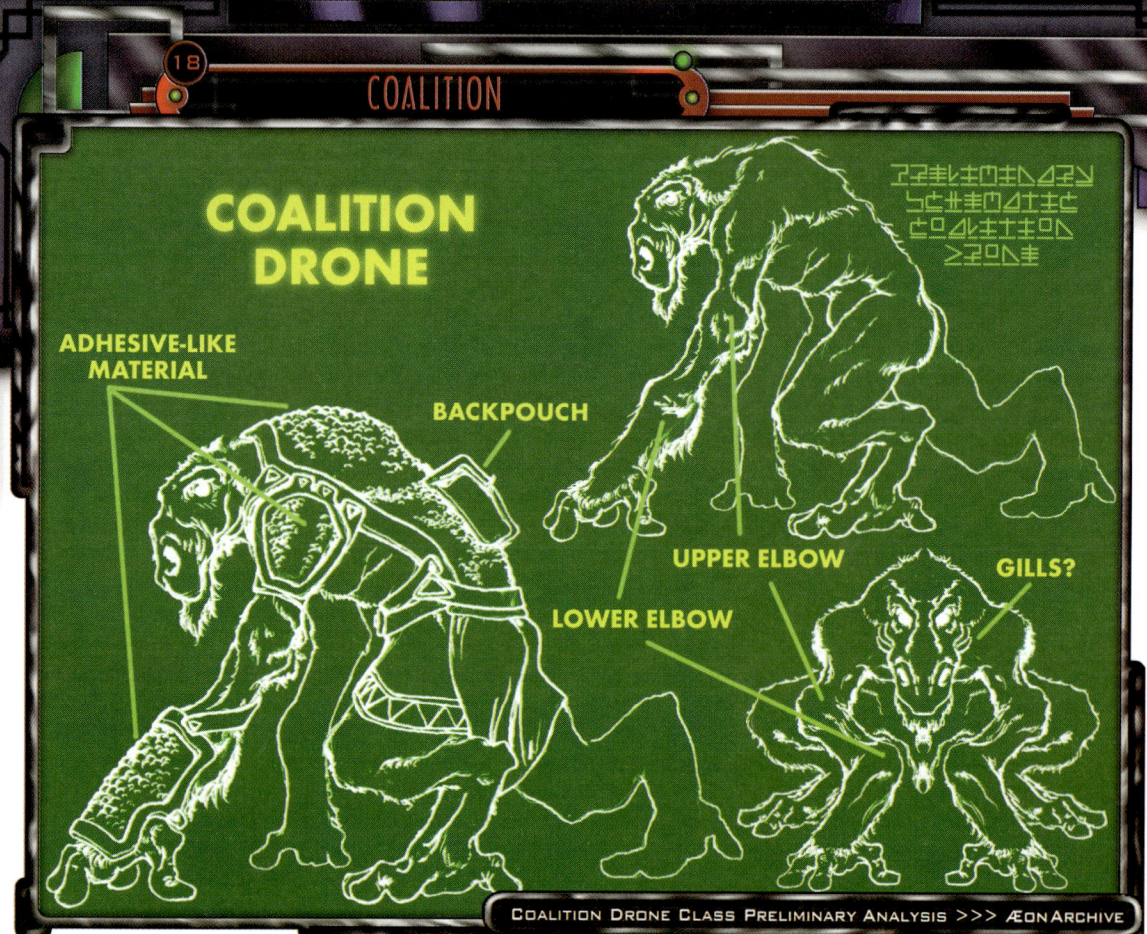

ADHESIVE-LIKE MATERIAL

BACKPOUCH

UPPER ELBOW

GILLS?

LOWER ELBOW

COALITION DRONE CLASS PRELIMINARY ANALYSIS >>> ÆON ARCHIVE

means of interaction between two species in the region of space from which the Coalition hails. As such, our first diplomats were met according to what the Coalition thought was time-honored diplomatic tradition. However, sexual practice here is brutal by human standards, and the communication barrier kept the Coalition from realizing what was going on until it was too late.

I noticed during our conversation that two drones engaged in what seemed to be coitus. The lead envoy confirmed my suspicions, and expressed concern that we might be upset. I reassured him that we were prepared to deal with customs far different from our own. While I'm still not happy with what happened to the *Yi*, I am prepared to believe that it was an accident.

After this initial conversation, the lead envoy assigned each member of my staff a drone, which is apparently customary for distinguished visitors. Rooms had already been prepared for our staff. The envoy requested

that we not venture outside a designated area, to prevent further misunderstandings.

All went very well in the following week. The three envoys assigned to speak with us were as helpful as could be. Certain topics seemed to be taboo to them for religious reasons, but otherwise they were very forthcoming. I was concerned at first that the rooms prepared for us would be unsatisfactory, but the drones and the vaguely ursoid mechanics the *Yi* report called "sasqs" made the changes we required both quickly and easily. Coalition races seem to work together extremely well; I think the drones are more intelligent than I first surmised. They do walk on two legs when necessary. In any case, we've been able to move most of our operations over to the ark.

The technology we've seen is completely hardtech. Biotech was unknown to the Coalition races before the *Yi* expedition, and they're very interested in the concept. Earth should consider biotech a prime commodity when dealing with these races. Their hardtech is approximately as sophisticated as ours, although our scientists tell me theirs has developed in fascinating different directions. We are extremely interested in learning their method of propulsion, but the Coalition seems unwilling to discuss it at this time. I have to note that much of the work that we relegate to machines is carried out by various domesticated animals here.

Labor and work [divisions are organized along] strict racial grounds. The envoys claim this regimentation is voluntary and natural. Given Earth's history, I am suspicious of the claim, but I must try to remind myself that these races have their own cultures — our rules do not apply. I will watch carefully for signs of dissent, though.

Datapod Dump Two

— Molly Irvingson, Ambassador in Chief, Second UN Expedition to the Coalition

The remainder of our first month on the Coalition ship continued to be productive.

Kohl was restationed approximately 100,000 kilometers from the space ark for ease of access, while *Pandora* remains at a distance. This datadump summarizes xenobiological and psionic reports, with more of my own notes at the end.

>>> text lost <<<

We requested permission to dissect one of the drones early on. The envoys were somewhat taken aback by the request; it seems that the drones *are* a semi-intelligent race. However, after some internal discussion, they agreed to provide a dead drone for our studies, along with several members of their food species — quadrupeds a little smaller than a horse, which I've nicknamed "cattle." It seems appropriate, as their cattle are also beasts of burden.

Autopsies revealed nothing of particular note from a diplomatic perspective. However, detailed DNA analysis shows that the drones and cattle are related to a very close degree; more so than, say, chimpanzees and

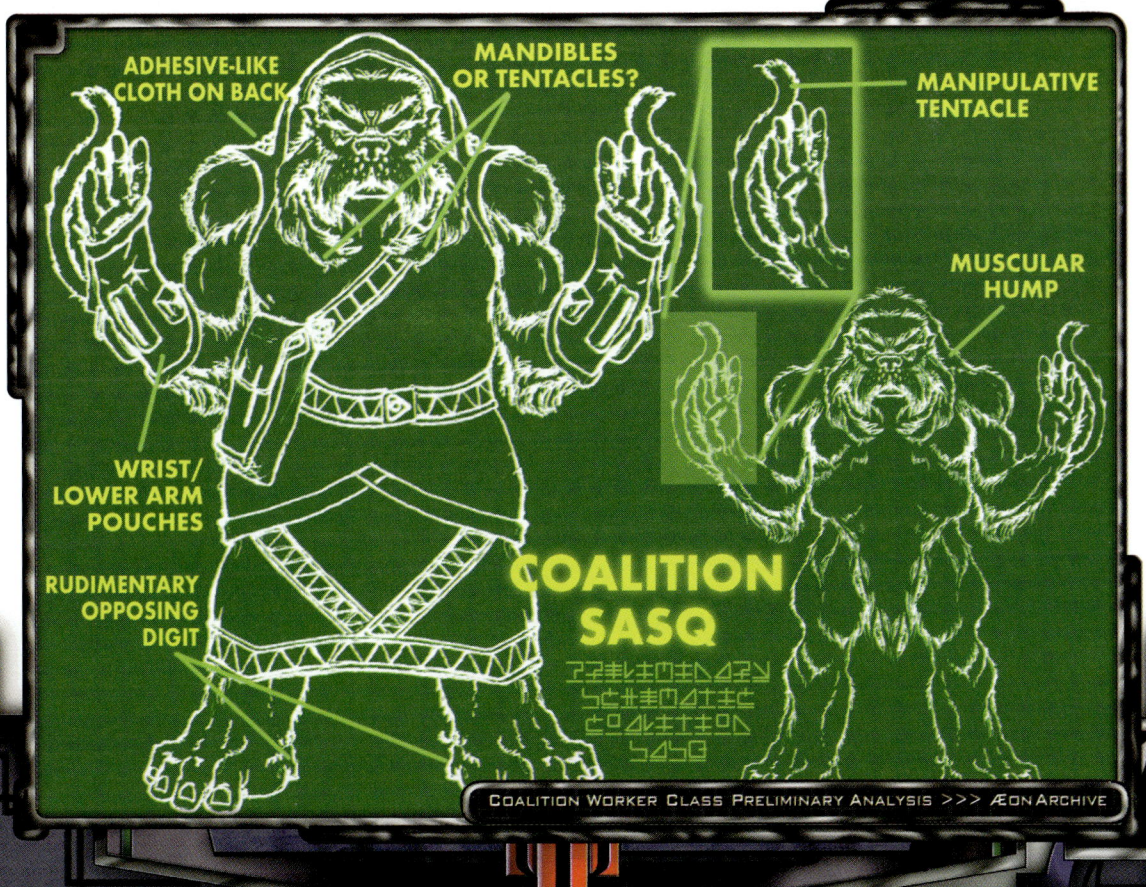

ADHESIVE-LIKE CLOTH ON BACK
MANDIBLES OR TENTACLES?
MANIPULATIVE TENTACLE
MUSCULAR HUMP
WRIST/ LOWER ARM POUCHES
RUDIMENTARY OPPOSING DIGIT

COALITION SASQ

COALITION WORKER CLASS PRELIMINARY ANALYSIS >>> ÆON ARCHIVE

humans. I've discussed this with the envoys, who explain that this is the result of their aforementioned "diplomatic custom."

Our xenobiologists speculate that the old "spore" theory — a common origin for galactic life spread by some sort of space spore — might be close to the truth where the Coalition originates. It seems a reasonable explanation for what we've found. Doctor Lundgard is lobbying for permission to sample envoy tissue by "accident." I'm inclined to agree if he can come up with a discreet method of extraction. This expedition wasn't expected to resolve any xenobiological mysteries. It's wonderful that we're finding out so much.

The autopsies revealed unusually large scent glands beneath the skin of both races. The scents they produce are, as best we can tell, pheromones — their scents trigger instinctual responses in beings that smell them. I say "beings" because these pheromones seem to be effective on humans as well as the Coalition. The drones' scent leaves one disinterested >>> text lost <<< and the cattle's scent leaves one feeling somewhat satiated after eating, or hungry if you haven't. Strange as it sounds, I've wondered how the cattle taste.

We speculate that the [racial division of labor is the result of] natural pheromone secretions. For example, the drones are natural servants, and as such, you never notice them when they are not needed. With all this in mind, the *Yi* crew reports of "unavoidable attraction" begin to make sense. The envoys confirmed our suspicions; this subconscious pheromone production is another reason why we've been asked to remain in a small area aboard the space ark. The Coalition is unlikely to ever be able to interact with humanity as easily as the Qin do, I fear, but we may yet find ways to work together.

We've found no traces of noetic ability on board the ark. Joanna Tzavelas, our best clairvoyant, scanned for noetic activity throughout our portion of the space ark and found nothing. Some of our psionic staff, particularly our Legion guards, provided the envoys with *ad hoc* [demonstrations of psychokinesis] and other powers. While I'd have preferred not to display our abilities, we did discover that the envoys were unfamiliar with noetics — if their surprised and even shocked reactions were any indication.

More troublesome, though, were the faint traces of taint Ms. Tzavelas discovered toward the center of the ark. Ivan Gullichsen, another clairvoyant, confirmed the existence of taint the same day. A week later, the traces had faded. More on this later.

Very light telepathic scans yielded little of any use. The envoys are either apt at separating surface thought from internal contemplation, or are rather shallow. Judging from their diplomatic skill shown so far, I'd guess the former. We attempted deeper scans on the sasqs and drones, as well as the warrior caste, the "spinals." The spinals dream of battle, as one might guess from their razor-edged angles and menacing postures. Sasqs and drones, as far as we can tell, think mainly >>> text lost <<< [This discovery does] bear out the contention that the division of labor is natural.

As far as diplomatic talks go, we're still in the preliminary phases. I'm content with this pace; the more time we have to study the Coalition, the better. I wonder if the envoys are really the guiding hands behind the Coalition. While their racial specialization isn't as specific as that of, say, Earth insects, I'm unsure if diplomacy and leadership fall into the same category.

Perhaps I'm anthropomorphizing. Given the emphasis on intercourse in social relationships, maybe skillful interaction is seen as the primary component of leadership. It's been difficult for me accept the degree to which sex seems to be part of this culture. I haven't witnessed cross-racial intercourse yet, but the more usual sort is terribly common.

Speaking of racial issues, I've decided that if there really is a flavor of slavery to the racial divisions, it's long since been institu-

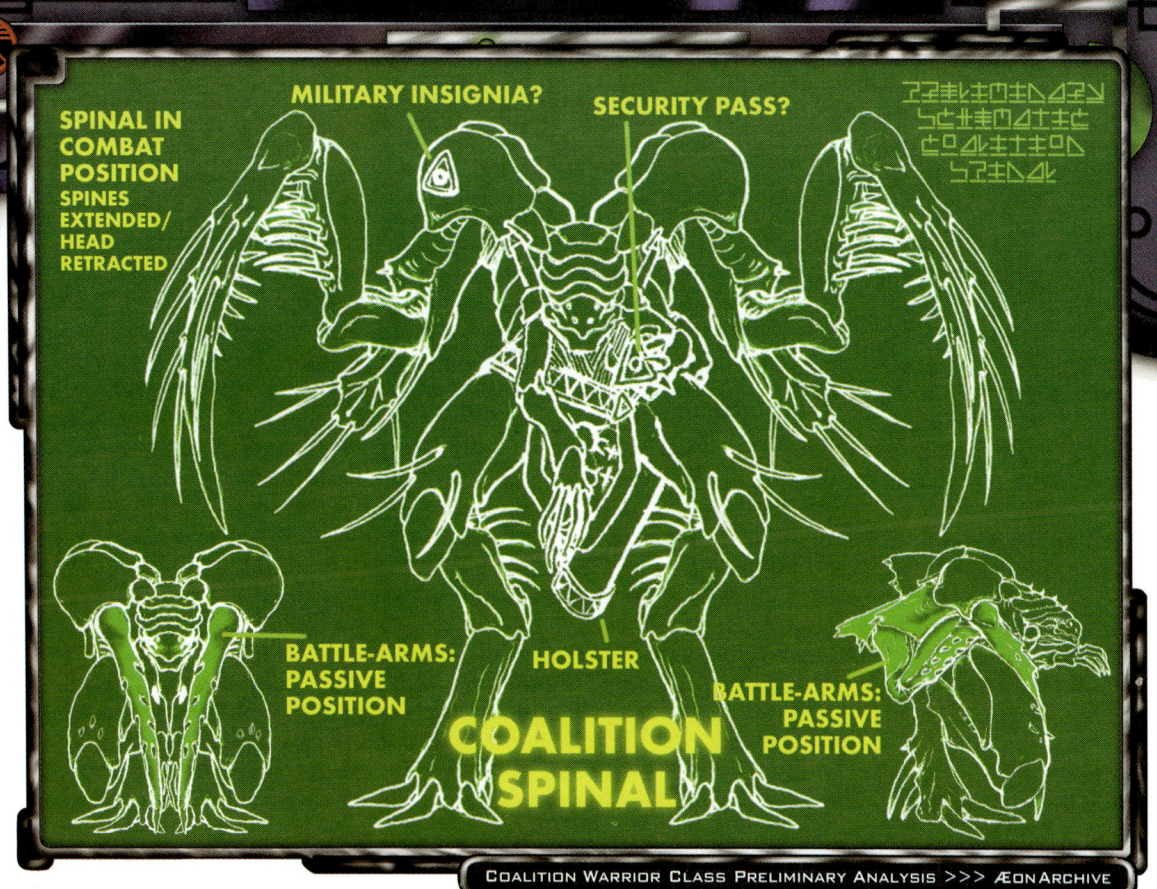

SPINAL IN COMBAT POSITION
SPINES EXTENDED/HEAD RETRACTED

MILITARY INSIGNIA?

SECURITY PASS?

BATTLE-ARMS: PASSIVE POSITION

HOLSTER

BATTLE-ARMS: PASSIVE POSITION

COALITION SPINAL

tionalized and has become unconscious. The envoys are unable to remember that form does not indicate function among humans. I am tall and skinny, thus the envoys constantly assume that all tall, skinny humans are diplomats. For some reason the envoys also treat females with an exaggerated respect, perhaps because of a similar appearance to a race we haven't encountered yet.

On the taint issue, I've decided two things: I'm going to request that Ms. Tzavelas perform a physical scan of the area where she detected taint. Second, depending on the results, I may send a small group of Legionnaires to investigate the matter personally. The envoys have not mentioned Aberrant attacks, and show no signs of taint themselves, but I am willing to risk this mission to get to the bottom of the matter. When I consider taint in conjunction with the speed with which the envoys learned English… the possibilities are alarming.

Datapod Dump Three
— General Luo Meng, Staff General, Second UN Expedition to the Coalition

Ambassador Irvingson is missing. As per mission protocol, I have taken command of the ambassadorial staff, and we will proceed with the mission. We have not yet moved to a combat footing, as the reasons for the ambassador's disappearance are not yet known.

She vanished three days after the marine mission to investigate the taint. The circumstances are unclear. The last person [to see her was] >>> text lost <<<

The envoys express polite concern for the ambassador's status, and suggest that she might have ventured beyond the human-designated area. It's possible — the ambassador is known to be impulsive — but unlikely. The envoys report that their patrols have found no sign of her. We'll continue to investigate.

In the meantime, diplomacy continues under my reluctant supervision. I've noted in the

REPORT: RECON OF COALITION SPACE ARK

— Captain William Donney, UN Military [detached duty to the Coalition Expedition]

At 0500 LST, which we estimate to be the time of lowest activity for Coalition members, a four-person field team set out from our quarantine zone aboard the ark. In addition to myself, the team consisted of Corporals Jacqueline Winters and Leon Savarese, both combat experts, and Ivan Gullichsen, a clairvoyant. Corporal Savarese is a talented psion who comes to us after a distinguished service with the Legions.

Mr. Gullichsen maintained a scan during the entire mission, which allowed us to avoid almost all contact with Coalition members. While we passed numerous drones, we did not see members of any sentient Coalition species. Gullichsen's abilities were also a great help in navigating the ark's corridors. They proved to be >>> text lost <<< [The space ark] proper is more reminiscent of a house that's grown over the years than a specifically designed vessel.

As we approached the center of the ship, we saw more of the iconography previously identified as religious in nature. Gullichsen finally detected taint directly in front of a large hatchway bearing a number of symbols, some religious and some, as yet, unclassified. The taint residue was consistent with the passage of an Aberrant. Gullichsen probed into the area beyond, which he claims was unlike any of our preconceptions of a spacecraft. He described it as a network of caverns which were individually as large as 10 meters high and more than 100 meters across. Here and there, he also >>> text lost <<< He ceased probing upon detecting strong signs of taint in one cavern.

We returned to our own zone with no incident. The entire mission took approximately two hours.

logs that I would prefer to withdraw and reassess, but mission parameters don't permit that course of action. The entire expedition is on yellow alert. I've taken the precaution of asking our technicians to design several sets of respirators capable of countering drone and cattle pheromones, assuming that other Coalition races might >>> text lost <<< [I have] half the diplomatic staff wearing the things, with the others as control subjects. Daily reports from protected personnel are far more cautious, on average, than those from unprotected personnel. I've ordered the scientific staff to take samples of air from rooms containing envoys.

Dr. Lundgard has also found that envoy DNA is congruent with drone and cattle DNA to the 99th percentile. The different species making up the Coalition are far more closely related than the envoys would have us believe. None of us are sure what to make of this, but the Coalition is clearly keeping a number of secrets from us.

Datapod Dump Four

— Captain Mary Palacio, Leviathan *Pandora*

This is what you need to know.

The Coalition is not many races; it's one race, bred [into a hundred] subspecies for functionality, ruled by things at the center of the ark. We've come to call these things "breeders."

General Luo spent a week in diplomacy, trying to find out where the taint was coming from, what the envoys were hiding and where the ambassador vanished to. The general is a stubborn man; he finally gave up and asked the envoys outright.

The envoys tried to delay. They admitted that the Coalition has a central subrace >>> text lost <<< [and that members of our] first expedition became raw genetic breeding material. It's what the bastards have done with every other race they've encountered for thousands of years. They trotted out the product of their breeders and our first expedition — a half-human, half-envoy monstrosity that looked about 10 years old, but with eyes >>> text lost <<< Everyone was wearing respirators by then, which was a good thing. The creature was pumping out pheromones twice as potent to humans as those of the envoys. General Luo demanded to have the creature, along with any other human genetic samples the Coalition had. The envoys refused, and a fight broke out.

We've been battling the ark for three days. She has "children"; a swarm of what I'd call fighters engaged our frigates and *Pandora*. A lucky shot took out our jump capacity along with >>> text lost <<< [General Luo fought a holding action] inside the space ark while a marine detachment fought toward the center of the ship, looking for answers.

God, did they find them.

There's a lot of human genetic material on board — or should I say formerly human? *Aberrants* got here not too long ago. There are breeding chambers full of them! Our troops broke through, got a look at what was inside, and fled as if Divis Mal himself was on their heels. Who knows, he might be here.

General Luo was holding well enough against the spinals until Aberrant reinforcements showed up. Then there was no hope >>> text lost <<< In the end, he got the civilians off, giving up the *Chelsea*'s firepower in order to get them to *Pandora*. We haven't heard from the General since. There's only one reasonable assumption.

As I said earlier, our Tesser drive is ruined. We're only getting enough power to send this message. *Kohl* is dead; not returning our hails. We're going to try to limp away from this hell in normal space. The Coalition ship is incredibly fast, but it steers like a cow, even compared to a Leviathan. We won't make it back to Earth any time soon, but at least we won't be in Coalition hands.

Remember us.

LAST VID FROM SECOND UN COALITION EXPEDITION >>> ÆON ARCHIVE

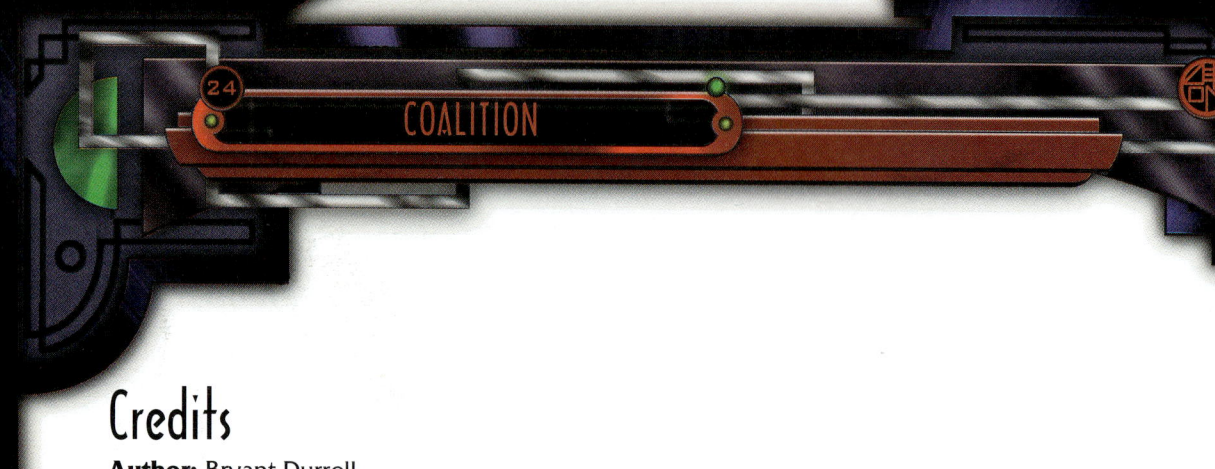

Credits

Author: Bryant Durrell
Developers: Andrew Bates and Ken Cliffe
Concept Suggested by: Scott Nimmo
Editor: Carl Bowen
Graphic Stuff: Richard Thomas
Cover Art: Jeff Holt, David Robyn Seeley and Richard Thomas
Artists: Rob Dixon, Jeff Holt, Brian Snoddy and Richard Thomas

Author Dedication: To Eric Hargin, John Abbe and Gretchen Shanrock, for helping me learn to roleplay.

WHITE WOLF
GAME STUDIO

735 PARK NORTH BLVD.
SUITE 128
CLARKSTON, GA 30021
USA

© 1998 White Wolf Publishing, Inc. All rights reserved. Reproduction without the written permission of the publisher is expressly forbidden, except for the purposes of reviews, and for blank character sheets, which may be reproduced for personal use only. White Wolf is a registered trademark of White Wolf Publishing, Inc. All rights reserved. Trinity, Trinity Universe, Trinity Field Report and Trinity Field Report Alien Races are trademarks of White Wolf Publishing, Inc. All rights reserved. All characters, names, places and text herein are copyrighted by White Wolf Publishing, Inc.

The mention of or reference to any company or product in these pages is not a challenge to the trademark or copyright concerned.

This book uses science fiction for settings, characters and themes. All science fiction, geopolitical situations and psi-related elements are fiction and are intended for entertainment purposes only. Reader discretion is advised.

Check out White Wolf online at
http://www.white-wolf.com; alt.games.whitewolf and rec.games.frp.storyteller
PRINTED IN CANADA.